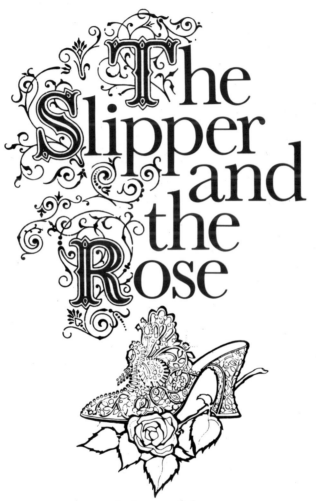

The Slipper and the Rose

Adapted by
BRYAN FORBES
From an original script by
BRYAN FORBES, ROBERT B. SHERMAN
and RICHARD M. SHERMAN

NAMARA PUBLICATIONS / QUARTET BOOKS

This book is for
Sarah and Emma
with love

LIBRARY OF CONGRESS CATALOG CARD
NUMBER: LC 76-39611

First published in the United States of America 1976
by Quartet Books Inc.
a Member of the Namara Group, 55 Park Avenue, New York, N.Y. 10016, USA.

First published in 1976 by
Namara Publications Limited
18b Wellington Court, Knightsbridge, London SW1X 7PL
and Quartet Books Limited
27 Goodge Street, London W1P 1FD

Design by Michael Jarvis
Drawings by Shirley Curzon
ISBN 0 704 32127 0

Printed by Gavin Martin Ltd, Surrey, England.

It was a hard Winter that year. Not since the day when the old King had succeeded to the throne had the people of Euphrania known such cold. Birds were frozen to the branches of the trees and although the children, braving the bitter winds, enjoyed skating on the frozen rivers and lakes of the small kingdom, their parents sat huddled by the ever-burning stoves longing for the Spring to come.

It was said that if you climbed to the top of the castle where the King lived you could see every corner of the land he ruled over. It was a country of mountains and pine forests, a country of legends and mysteries, undisturbed for countless centuries.

Had you been brave enough to climb to the topmost turret of the castle on the day this story begins, you would have seen the sad sight of a funeral procession setting out from a house that sat on an island in the middle of a lake.

This house belonged to a rich merchant, a man whose life had been full of woe. His first wife had died giving birth to a daughter and in later years, unable to bear the loneliness, he took a second wife. This was a widow who had long cherished the thought of sharing the rich merchant's beautiful home. She already had two daughters of her own, Isobella and Palatine, proud and spiteful girls who had inherited their mother's greed.

Even before the wedding bells had ceased ringing they made the poor merchant's life a misery, and he saw his hard-earned fortune scattered like chaff in an Autumn wind. He was a kind man at heart, always ready to see the best in people, and he suffered in silence.

He doted upon his own daughter who went by the unusual name of Cinderella. While he was alive he protected Cinderella as best he could from the rages and insults poured upon her by her Stepmother and Step-sisters.

Now, on the Winter's day when our story begins, he could protect her no longer, for the funeral procession setting out across the drawbridge of the house on an island on the lake was his.

Black-plumed horses fretted and stamped in the shafts of three black sleighs, anxious to return to their warm stables. There were few mourners, for since his marriage to her his second wife had allowed few visitors to the house and his once numerous friends had stopped calling.

The coffin was a simple one, for even in death his wife denied him any comfort. She and her two daughters had not even bothered to provide a wreath for his last journey – the only flowers that accompanied him to his snowy grave were a bunch of blood-red roses that Cinderella had obtained from the gardener.

The procession passed out of the town and moved slowly across the barren countryside, the mourners huddled together against the cold.

The mountains in the background were shrouded with the clouds that held the next fall of snow, and from the direction of these mountains came four horsemen.

The two leading horsemen carried the pennants of the King's only son and heir to the throne, the Prince Edward of Euphrania. He and his Companion-at-Arms, John, were returning from a journey far beyond the borders of the kingdom.

The Prince's Guards dipped their pennants in salute as the funeral procession crossed their path, but the Prince did not look up, for he, too, was heavy of heart. Thus he remained unaware of Cinderella's existence.

Trumpets sounded as the look-outs on the castle battlements saw Prince Edward's approach. Their echoes were still dying away when he strode into the vast entrance hall. Servants hurried to disrobe him and provide a warming goblet of wine.

'Why do they have to sound so many trumpets?' the Prince asked. 'Why can't a Prince come home without fuss?'

'Presumably . . . because he *is* a Prince, sire,' John said.

'Other people can sneak in the back way, unannounced,

which is how it should be.'

He stood in front of the great fireplace.

'A Prince's lot is nothing more than a bore. Now, you mark my words, John. Before you've counted to ten, through that door, with the odious punctuality of our neighbour's much-vaunted, recently-invented, hideously-irritating cuckoo clock, will come our dear and loyal subject, the ever-unctuous Lord High Chamberlain.'

John started to count softly. And sure enough, by the time he had counted seven the Lord Chamberlain had made his expected appearance, bowing low – so low in fact that his staff of office scraped the ground.

'Your Royal Highness . . .'

'My Lord High Chamberlain, what an unexpected pleasure . . .'

'Welcome home, Your Royal Highness. I am commanded by His Majesty the King, your father, and Her Majesty the Queen, your mother . . .'

The Prince interrupted him. 'Yes, yes, now don't exhaust yourself, I am acquainted with them, you know. How are my doting parents?'

The Lord Chamberlain swelled with self-importance.

'Their Majesties are naturally most anxious to hear such glad tidings as I am sure you bear concerning the reasons for your recent absence from the Court . . .'

He failed to notice the look which Prince Edward exchanged with John at this point.

'. . . namely the matter of your acceptance of and betrothal to the Princess Selena of Carolsfeld. Indeed, in anticipation of the long-awaited good news His Majesty has seen fit to make you a Knight Grand Cross of the Most Illustrious Order of Saint David the Blessed Martyr . . .'

'Which is usually awarded posthumously,' the Prince observed dryly. 'A suitable honour as it happens, for the matter of my betrothal is very status quo . . . I did not find the lady of your choice to be my choice. We are returned as we departed.'

He handed his empty goblet to a servant. 'Come,' he said, 'let us break the sad news to my parents.'

The King and Queen were in the Throne Room where the King was playing his favourite game – a sort of Snakes and Ladders with page boys as the pieces. It was a complicated and, if the truth were known, very boring game, but the King liked it and what the King liked everybody else had to suffer. He always won because he always cheated, a habit which annoyed the Queen more than anything she could think of, which wasn't much.

The King was just about to throw the over-large dice when his son strode into the chamber.

'Ah!' he said. 'At last! Our dear son . . . we are . . . we are . . .' Words failed him, as they were often apt to do. He turned to the Queen. 'What are we?'

'Delighted?' the Queen suggested.

'Yes, we are delighted to see you return. I have something for you to celebrate the occasion.'

He handed the dice to the Queen, who in turn handed it to her Lady-in-Waiting, and the sheer weight of it nearly broke that good woman's wrists.

The King advanced to the centre of the Throne Room and beckoned to an aide.

'Kneel, sir,' he said to his son.

'Your Majesty . . . Father,' the Prince said, 'this is most embarrassing.'

'I command you to kneel, sir.'

'I don't deserve anything. I haven't earned it.'

'Nobody earns this. It's given because I'm the King and I like it . . . where's my sword?'

The sword was produced and the King, who loved the sound of his own voice, began the ceremony.

'Let it be known to all here present that by Our command His Royal Highness, the Prince Edward Charles Albert George James Richard Augustus Philip, has received Our gracious favour.'

At this point he dropped the sword, for he had been born with the curse of weak wrists. In the resulting confusion the Dowager Queen, who slept most of the day and sipped jasmine tea most of the night, awoke with a start.

'There's somebody in the room,' she shouted to nobody in particular; nobody in particular paid any attention, and a few moments later she was fast asleep again.

The King continued, 'From this day henceforth the Prince my son shall be entitled to be known as a Knight Grand Cross of the Most Illustrious Order of Saint David the Blessed Martyr.'

He took the award from an aide and placed it around the Prince's neck. It was an extremely ugly award and also a very heavy one. That was why very few people liked to receive it.

The King kissed his son on both cheeks.

'That's the part I like best,' the Queen remarked. 'I sometimes give medals to a whole regiment.'

'Good,' said the King after the embrace. 'Very touching ceremony.'

'Most touching, sire,' the Lord Chamberlain echoed.

The King gave him a very Royal look. 'Sycophant,' he said – it was one of the few words he could ever remember.

At this moment there was a sudden disturbance at the far end of the Throne Room and the whole Court turned to see who had caused it.

It was the Duke of Montague, first cousin to the Prince and next in line to the throne. The thought that Cousin Montague might somehow succeed to the throne kept the King awake at night, and that was why he was so anxious that his son should find a suitable bride, marry and have children.

Cousin Montague dressed in a rather flamboyant fashion.

His hair was tightly curled and he looked rather like a large bird as he advanced towards the Prince and proclaimed his greeting in his loud and irritating voice.

'Congratulations, dear cousin, I heard all the trumpets.'

The King turned away to continue his game, for he found it difficult to be polite to Cousin Montague.

'You're cheating again,' the Queen said.

'Kings never cheat. They adapt to circumstances, but they never cheat.'

The Prince came between them.

'You see how I'm placed,' the King said. 'Accused in the presence of the Court by my own wife.'

'Father, by your leave, this is serious . . .'

'Of course it's serious. I shall probably concede the game. It's a Royal failing to be unsporting.'

'I meant, father, that I have something serious to say to you. I have given up all thoughts of marrying the Princess Selena.'

The whole Court fell silent.

'You what, sir?'

'The match, father, was of your making, not of mine. Even so, as a dutiful son, I honoured your wishes. I journeyed far beyond our borders to pay my respects to the lady and see for myself.'

'And she was fair, was she not?' asked the King.

The Prince, who was a polite young man, lowered his voice.

'Indeed, sire. Perhaps pale rather than fair. A sickly lady, sire. Given to much swooning and taking of the vapours.'

'All women swoon,' said the King with a look at his wife. 'They know it's expected of them.'

'Some swoon more than others, sire, and swooning to excess is not a quality I greatly admire.'

For the first time in the conversation the King took notice.

'You mean she refused you?'

'No, father. She could not refuse me because I did not offer,' the Prince said patiently. He glanced around the Court and lowered his voice yet again, so that the King had to lean forward to catch his words.

'In your natural anxiety to see me wed before my cousin Montague and thus ensure your House's succession, you perhaps placed too much trust in the portrait painters of Carolsfeld.'

The Prince mentioned this because of course in the days before the camera had been invented people had to rely on oil paintings for a likeness.

'The likeness was no likeness,' the Prince continued. 'Indeed, since you force me to the discourtesy, the lady was bald, sire, her golden tresses false, her mouth crabbed with age, sire, and devoid of teeth. In short, sire, she left much to be desired.'

'Extraordinary,' said the King.

'Father,' his son persisted, 'it's a small thing and doubtless very irritating of me, but when I marry as needs I must one day, it will be for the convenience of love rather than . . . the convenience of convenience.'

'Love?' said the King.

'Did he say love?' said the Queen. 'How absurd.'

'What has love got to do with getting married? Find a mate, dear boy, find a mate.'

'Princess Susan, Princess Karen, Princess Kate,' said the Queen, naming but three.

'Love,' said the King, 'is highly over-rated and makes marriage complicated.'

Cousin Montague, who should have known better, but didn't, added his words of advice.

'Uncle, I couldn't have said it better myself. Well, I could, and in fact I will . . . Being married can't compare with being Royal.'

He would have said more, but the Lord Chamberlain took

him by the arm and led him away.

'We are bored with your defiance,' said the King. 'And what is more the future of our Royal line is at stake.'

He went and sat on his throne. The Queen sat on her throne.

'We are growing old, dear, and time is growing late,' she said.

The Prince remained silent. He was determined never to marry unless it be for love.

At that very moment Cinderella was returning home from her father's funeral. Her Stepmother and Stepsisters threw off their cloaks to reveal not dresses of mourning black but dresses such as one might wear to a party.

'What a relief,' her Stepmother said. 'That's over and done with.'

Cinderella stared at them in disbelief.

'Black is such an unbecoming colour,' Isobella pouted.

'Especially when one is young and pretty,' said Palatine.

Their mother stepped forward as Cinderella walked slowly towards the staircase.

'And where do you think you're going, child?'

'To my room, Stepmother,' Cinderella answered.

'*Your* room?'

The two sisters simpered. '*Her* room,' they echoed.

'All the rooms in this house are mine now,' their mother said. She stepped in front of Cinderella.

'Your father, my late husband, sadly missed by us all, is dead, child. Buried beneath the snow in the same grave as your mother. That is a double misfortune for you and now you must start a new life. Your father, as a token of his great love for me, saw fit to make a Will placing you in my care and protection.'

'My father never loved you. You tricked him,' Cinderella said.

'How dare you, child!'

'You tricked him!'

Her Stepmother took her roughly by the arm and pushed her towards the door which led down into the kitchen.

'Now, you listen to me and hear me well. Blood is thicker than a widow's tears, and I have two daughters of my own to support. Which situation forces me to make certain economies in the household. Is that not so, girls?'

'Yes, Mama,' her two daughters replied.

'Certain drastic economies, Mama,' Palatine said.

'Exactly. But being a woman of principle, I shall honour your father's last wishes and continue to provide a roof over your head . . . *below* stairs.'

Cinderella stared at her tormentors in disbelief.

'Oh, yes. And don't think you can find sympathy with the staff. The staff have been dismissed. You are now the staff.'

'To take orders instead of giving them,' said the smiling Isobella.

'Mostly from us,' added her sister.

'You will cook and you will carry. You will fetch and you will mend,' the Stepmother continued. 'Your father's Will allows and the Law upholds. So take your pick. Either accept your lot or go to the Orphanage.'

'They tell me, Cinderella, you can be awfully happy there,' said Isobella.

'And warm,' said Palatine. 'They sleep six to a bed. Not counting the rats.'

'Now don't tease,' their mother chided. 'It spoils your looks.'

She turned on Cinderella. 'Give me your cloak, child. You won't be needing it in the kitchen. Your first task is to make us some soup. Burying a husband is a cold business, and alas for me, I have now buried two.'

'Poor Mama' her daughters said in unison.

Their mother took Cinderella's fine cloak and tossed it to one side. Then she bundled Cinderella towards the door leading to the cellars and kitchens. 'Go along, and don't keep us waiting.'

Cinderella could no longer contain her tears as she went down the stone steps into the dank kitchen. A few hours before it had been a warm and friendly place – her father's staff had always served her with love – but now it seemed a prison from which she would never escape.

It was obvious that the cook and the maids had been dismissed at a moment's notice, for the once spotless kitchen looked abandoned. The fire was out, the copper pots and pans uncleaned, the dishes unwashed. On the table stood the remains of the last meal.

Cinderella sat on a stool by the dead fire. She shivered. Mice, who a few hours ago would not have dared to leave their nests, now nibbled at a round loaf on the table. Cinderella did not attempt to frighten them away, for something told her that they were likely to be her only friends and companions in the days to come.

The long hard Winter slowly gave way to the coming of Spring. The snows melted on the lower slopes of the mountains and the streams in the valleys ran with icy water, some of them overflowing their banks and flooding the rich pastures. Soon these were filled with wild flowers. It was the beginning of a new year for the people of Euphrania, and perhaps they hoped that this year would be different.

Certainly Cinderella wished that her life would change.
The start of Spring brought little comfort to her. She was
kept working night and day at the impossible task of satisfying
her Stepmother and her two Step-sisters – scrubbing, mending
and cooking from the moment she got up until she crawled
back into her miserable bed.

She had tamed the mice in the kitchen and they shared the
crumbs from her meals, but as anybody knows although they
are gentle little creatures, mice aren't the most talkative of
companions. Sometimes her loneliness became unbearable
and many a time she cried herself to sleep.

One morning she was out gathering firewood at an early
hour. The sun was out and the Spring flowers opened all
around her. She picked a small bunch and, on a sudden
impulse, ran across the fields to where her father and mother
lay buried. It was a simple cemetery which lay close to the
Royal Mausoleum.

Cinderella tidied the grave as best she could and laid her posy of flowers beside the iron headstone. She heard the sound of horsemen approaching and from instinct – for she was always fearful of discovery by her hateful Stepmother – she hid behind a tree.

The two horsemen were dressed in splendid clothes and as they drew closer she recognized the leading rider as the Prince Edward. Both riders dismounted outside the Mausoleum and went inside. Forgetting her own troubles for a moment, Cinderella slipped from hiding and made her way to the walls of the Mausoleum. She peeped through one of the iron grilles.

Inside, the Prince was explaining the various Royal tombs to his companion, John. Although not wishing to pry, Cinderella could not help overhearing their conversation.

'The first time they brought me here – it was part of my Royal education, you see – I was only knee-high to a tombstone, and they stood me in front of this and said: "That's yours, that's waiting for you".'

Cinderella shivered.

'Oh, very cheerful,' she heard John reply.

'Yes,' the Prince said, 'humour has never been the family's strong point. It's a sobering feeling, isn't it? No matter what I do, or don't do – no matter how I do it, or don't do it – my last appointment is here.'

His footsteps echoed around the marble walls as he walked from tomb to tomb of the ancient Kings of Euphrania and told John of their various exploits. There were good kings, bad kings, sane kings and mad kings, all buried beneath the same roof.

Cinderella stood on tip-toe to get a better look at the Prince, for she was anxious to see whether he was as handsome as people said. This proved to be her undoing, for the Prince turned and for one brief second they came face to face.

She ran from the spot as fast as she could.

'Who was that?' the Prince said.

'Sire?'

'A girl . . . there . . . she was hiding there.'

'I saw no one, sire,' John replied.

'I could have sworn . . . a servant girl.'

It was the Prince's turn to shiver. The Mausoleum seemed suddenly cold and uninviting.

'Oh, John, my friend . . . I know the end of my story, my story ends here, but not what comes in between. Will I ever live, before I die?'

Cinderella ran all the way home. The house seemed quiet as she raced across the drawbridge and into the hall-way. She gained the bottom of the stairs into the kitchen before a hand reached out to stop her and she was confronted by her angry Stepmother.

'So, you are returned at last, you wicked child. How dare you disobey me! Where have you been?'

'I only went to my parents' grave, Stepmother, to put some flowers there.'

'How touching. With flowers from my garden – stolen flowers.'

'No.'

'I say, "yes". I say you stole them. You are not only a liar, but a thief, and thieves, we know, must be punished. Come!'

She dragged Cinderella to another part of the kitchen and pushed her towards a mountain of vegetables – peas to be podded, potatoes, onions and turnips to be peeled, cabbages to be washed and shredded.

'There is no use in snivelling, you wretched child. This is your place and this is your task. We have guests for dinner tonight, important guests, so hurry about it. And for repaying my kindness with cunning and deceit, henceforth you will not dare to venture from this room without my permission, is that understood?'

'Yes,' Cinderella whispered.

'Then make a start and make amends.'

Cinderella could hardly see the pile of vegetables for tears. It was an impossible task for one person. She lifted one of the heavy iron pots from the fireplace and began.

Trumpets sounded as usual when the Prince returned to the castle. They served to remind him of his destiny.

'Tell me, John,' the Prince said. 'Have you ever wished you were in love?'

'Oh, yes, sire.'

'Often? I mean, as often as I wish it?'

'Well,' John said, 'I am in love.'

'How amazing! Who is she?'

'The Lady Caroline, sire.'

'The Lady-in-Waiting to my grandmother, that Lady Caroline?'

John nodded.

'Extraordinary,' the Prince said. 'Not extraordinarily extraordinary, of course, but I never guessed. Well, I'm delighted, you have my blessings. I must congratulate the lady.'

'No, please, don't do that, sire. It's kind of you but it would not be seemly.'

'How so?' said the Prince.

'My cause, alas, is a lost one.'

'The lady does not return your affections?'

'Oh, indeed. But it cannot be, you see – the protocol of the Court. I am what I am, a servant. Position, sire, position.'

'John, I am twice amazed,' said the Prince. 'I must be very dense. Am I?'

'No, of course not. You have your problems, I have mine.'

The Prince pondered this, as well he might, for as they talked the King was holding a meeting of the Star Council to discuss the ever-present problem of his only son's future.

All the King's Ministers were gathered together in the royal Library. A large map of Europe was spread out in front of the King. He leaned over the table to peer at it.

'Where are we?' the King said.

The Lord Chamberlain indicated Euphrania on the map. The King looked again.

'*That's* us? Are you sure this map is drawn to scale?'

'I believe so, Your Majesty.'

'Well, what have I been looking at all these years?' asked the King. 'I always thought that was us.'

He pointed to England. If the truth were known he had never been very good at geography, or mathematics, or spelling. In fact he had been the despair of the royal tutors.

The embarrassed silence was broken by a gentleman in a very splendid uniform.

'I always know the brown parts are the land, and the blue parts are the sea,' he mumbled to nobody in particular.

'Who is that?' whispered the King to the Lord Chamberlain.

'First Lord of the Navy, sire.'

'Have we got a Navy?' said the King.

'The Royal Barge, sire, on the lake.'

'Oh, yes. Well, remind me not to travel in it again.'

He turned back to his Ministers.

'So . . . allowing for errors in the cartographer's art, we are small in comparison with our neighbours. Although great in tradition and spirit, the fact remains that we are isolated, vulnerable and small. Therefore we have to have a plan. You are all aware of my son's reluctance to have a perfectly good wife chosen for him.'

All the heads nodded.

This was the Lord Chamberlain's moment. Taking the floor, he addressed the assembly in his most pompous voice.

'If you will allow me, Your Majesty, I have prepared a small paper.'

A few groans could be heard around the table, for it was well known that the Lord Chamberlain was fond of the sound of his own voice.

'I seek a proper balance, weighing what we lack against what we have to offer . . .'

'Oh, for goodness' sake don't talk in those boring diplomatic riddles, speak the King's Euphranian, man,' said the King.

'Forgive me, Your Majesty. I had in mind a celebration . . .'

'What are you going to celebrate?' said the King.

'A marriage, sire.'

The King looked puzzled. 'You getting married again? How extraordinary.'

'Not my marriage, sire. The Prince Edward's.'

'Well, we'd all like to celebrate that, that's what we're gathered here to talk about,' said the King. 'I sometimes think I'm surrounded by idiots.'

'This time, Your Majesty, I have a new idea. Something the Prince Edward will not be able to resist. I thought a Ball . . .'

Several of the Ministers woke up at this point.

'A Great Ball,' the Lord Chamberlain continued. 'The Greatest Ball that has ever been known. And to it we invite every eligible Princess in Europe and even beyond. We will make such preparations as will dazzle our enemies and divide them . . . for protocol will not allow them to declare war while they are guests in our midst.'

He handed the King a list of possible Princesses to choose from.

'I am convinced that the Prince, with them in the presence of the whole Court, will do his duty.'

The King pondered the suggestion for a few moments, then got to his feet.

'I shall make a Royal Decision,' he said. 'Taking this idea – and improving upon it, of course – I shall plan every detail to ensure its success. I am talking about diplomacy, protocol.'

'Indeed, indeed,' said the Lord Chamberlain.

The King strode up and down the Library like a General on the eve of battle.

'We must be protocoligorically correct,' he pronounced. 'We've a system to protect. Let us consult the Rules and Regulations.'

Various heavy books were produced from the dusty Library shelves and the King and his Ministers bent over them.

The planning for the Great Ball was under way.

Of course Cinderella, and indeed the Prince, knew nothing of this.

Alone in her dark kitchen Cinderella was still peeling and preparing the vegetables, and it was quite obvious that she would never finish in time.

There was a sudden knock at the door.

Puzzled, Cinderella listened, and the knock came again.

She got up and slowly walked to the door. She never had any visitors.

Opening the door, she was confronted by a complete stranger – a woman, simply dressed and carrying a basket. She had a kind face.

'Well, now,' the woman said . . . 'Were you expecting me?'

'No,' said Cinderella. 'I wasn't expecting anybody.'

The woman frowned. 'That's funny,' she said. 'You should have felt something. I must be losing my touch.' Then she smiled, and her smile seemed to lighten the darkest corners of the kitchen.

'Do you mind if I come in and warm my feet by your fire? I've been travelling a long way.'

'Well, I'm not supposed to talk to anybody,' Cinderella said. 'Or see anybody . . . but, yes, of course, you're welcome to share my fire, such as it is, though I'd be obliged if you didn't stay too long . . .'

The strange woman seated herself by the side of the miserable fire while Cinderella continued her task.

'Please excuse me if I don't stop working,' she said to the woman. 'I have to finish all these and I'm very slow.'

'Yes, well,' the woman said, 'there are more ways than one of shelling peas.'

Unobserved by Cinderella she turned away and poked out her tongue at the fire. It immediately blazed into comforting life.

'Live down here on your own, do you?' the woman asked Cinderella.

'I do now,' Cinderella said.

'Yes. Things have changed. But that doesn't mean to say they won't change again.' She smiled, and not for the first time Cinderella noticed that her smile was the warmest she had ever seen on any face.

'I get around quite a bit, you know.'

'It must be nice to travel,' Cinderella said, scraping yet another potato.

'Yes and no. I sometimes wish I could settle in one place, but there's never enough time. I'd like somewhere cosy, with a dog to keep me company. I expect your dog is a great comfort to you.'

'My dog?' Cinderella said. 'I haven't got a dog.'

'Isn't he yours?'

She pointed to the other end of the kitchen, and there, lying on his side on the stone floor, was a scruffy-looking little dog. He wagged his tail as Cinderella exclaimed in surprise.

'How . . . Where did he come from?'

'He came in when I came in,' the woman said.

Forgetting her task, Cinderella jumped up and rushed to the dog. He turned over onto his back as though asking her to tickle his tummy, which is a dog's way of telling you that he wants to be friends.

'What am I going to do with him?'

'Why don't you keep him?' the woman said. 'He'll take care of himself . . . he's an old hand at that. He seems to like you.'

'Oh, I love him,' Cinderella said, 'it's just that I'm so worried about what my Stepmother will say.'

At that precise moment there was a shout from the hallway above. 'Cinderella!'

'There she is now,' Cinderella whispered. 'Oh dear, and I haven't finished.'

'Well, I'll be off,' the woman said. 'I've seen all I want to see. You just take care of him.'

Cinderella gathered the little dog into her arms.

'I'll have to hide you,' she said, and looked around for a safe place. Just a second before her Stepmother opened the heavy door at the top of the stairs she had managed to hide the dog under the covers of her bed.

'I hope you've been hard at work, child . . .' She did not

get a chance to complete the sentence. Her mouth dropped open and she stared past Cinderella. Cinderella followed her look and now it was her turn to be amazed.

The kitchen had been transformed. The fire was blazing, the pots and pans shone as though they were brand new, the floor had been swept, but most miraculously of all, the mountain of vegetables had disappeared. Every potato was peeled, every carrot scraped, every cabbage prepared. They were all arranged in neat piles on the spotless table as regular as the King's Guards on parade.

Her Stepmother stepped forward, unable to believe her eyes.

'Well . . .' she said, finally. 'Well, I see . . . I see I shall have to give you more to do next time.' She went back up the stairs without another word.

Left to herself again, Cinderella pinched herself to see whether she was awake instead of dreaming. Then she took the little dog from his hiding place and cuddled him.

'What do you make of all that?' she said, with another look towards the table.

If the truth were known, the little dog knew more than she guessed, but he was sworn to secrecy and contented himself with licking Cinderella's face.

Meanwhile, at the Palace, Prince Edward had just learned of his father's plans for the Great Ball. He was furious.

'I totally refuse to take part in such an embarrassing charade,' he said, striding up and down the Throne Room in front of his parents.

Outside the doors of the Throne Room the Lord Chamberlain and several of the King's Ministers were listening. They heard the King say: 'But I've decreed it', and the Prince reply: 'Then you must un-decree it. The very idea of throwing a Ball and inviting a selection of royal wallflowers to vie for my hand in marriage is utterly repulsive, degrading to all concerned.'

The Lord Chamberlain shook his head. He was a worried man. Things weren't going as he had planned.

'I am your father and I am the King . . . and this suggestion seems perfectly reasonable to me. We've invited every eligible Princess in the Almanack . . . and it's a question of duty.'

'Ah!' said the Prince. He stopped pacing and faced his father. 'I knew you'd come to that sooner or later. Father, I have never questioned that it is my bounden duty to take a wife and ensure the royal succession . . . but that doesn't mean that I have to be party to and judge a cattle show. Who ever heard of such a thing!'

The Queen had never seen her son look so angry. She went and sat on her Throne.

'I mean,' the Prince continued. 'A bridefinding-Ball, can't you just imagine it? Me, the royal fatted-calf . . . with every maiden having a good laugh at my expense . . . it's . . . it's nauseating and I won't go through with it.'

The family argument was interrupted by the unwelcome arrival of Cousin Montague who came bounding in without knocking.

'I've just heard the news,' he exclaimed as he came forward to kiss the Queen's hand. 'Dear Aunt, dear Uncle, is it true? The buzz is that you're going to invite a whole nursery of nubile delicacies to a Ball.'

'Some other time, nephew,' said the King. 'We're busy now.'

'But you can't keep me in suspense, you just can't, Uncle. I mean, I realize I won't have first pick, but that doesn't matter to me, because I'm not proud . . . I'm just desperate.'

'We're all desperate,' said the King wearily.

'So, it's true then. Oh, how exciting! I must decide what to wear . . . high heels, I think, to give me added stature.' He turned to his cousin. 'The moment you've made your choice, Edward, I shall unleash myself.'

'I've already made my choice,' Prince Edward replied. 'As far as I'm concerned you can have your pick of the lot.'

Before they could continue this conversation any further the doors at the far end of the Throne Room were flung open and the Lord Chamberlain and his Ministers walked in solemn procession towards the King and Queen. Their faces were grave.

'Your Majesty,' the Lord Chamberlain said, bowing low, 'I bring grave tidings. Carolsfeld has mobilized. There is talk of war.'

The Ministers all nodded in agreement.

'War?' said the Queen, getting to her feet in some alarm.

The Lord Chamberlain bowed again. 'As Your Majesties' Senior Minister of State it is my solemn duty to advise you that the situation is critical. The news that His Royal Highness the Prince Edward saw fit to decline the hand of the Princess Selena in marriage was ill-received.'

'True,' echoed one of the Ministers.

The King came slowly forward and appealed to his son.

'Edward, I beseech you – not as a father, but as your Monarch – reconsider before it is too late. Put aside your personal feelings, the whole country looks to you to make an alliance through the marriage bed . . . Do as I did when I took your mother . . . I closed my eyes and thought of Euphrania.'

The Prince looked from one to the other. He had no choice. He had lost the day. Preparations for the Great Ball would go forward.

First of all he had to pose for a new portrait. Sixteen of the finest artists in Euphrania were summoned to the Palace and set to work. The sixteen finished portraits were dispatched to the far corners of the earth, taken to each of the foreign Princesses by messengers who rode night and day, changing their exhausted horses at frequent intervals. Not all of them were welcomed at the end of their journeys and sad to relate, some of them never lived to return to their native land.

The King and the Lord Chamberlain counted up their losses and successes in the Library.

'Six out of sixteen,' the King said in his most reflective mood. 'I think that's a fair average, don't you?'

'Yes, Your Majesty. Perhaps not quite the breadth of choice we at first envisaged . . .'

Because he was a king, the King was never at a loss for words. 'Well, we'll invite all the local nobility as well, we don't want the ballroom looking half empty, that would never do. We can always raise the taxes to pay for it . . . in fact, I shall invent a new tax, a tax on snobbery. They'll all pay that.'

'Brilliant, Your Majesty, brilliant,' the Lord Chamberlain said.

'Don't overdo it, don't overdo it,' said the King. 'You'll be paying it too . . .'

Excitement spread throughout the land as news of the preparations for the Great Ball became known. Those people lucky enough to receive one of the royal invitations immediately set to work to out-dazzle their neighbours.

Cinderella's Stepmother rushed to tell her two daughters that their invitation had arrived. The invitation included Cinderella, but the evil woman didn't reveal this – she had no intention of letting Cinderella go to the ball and possibly outshine her two darlings.

Upon being told the news, the two Step-sisters simpered and swooned. Primping and congratulating themselves, utterly convinced that the Prince would have difficulty in choosing between them, they paid no heed to poor Cinderella who was busy as usual scrubbing the staircase. They pushed past her, kicking over her bucket in their anxiety to snatch the invitation out of their mother's hands and read it for themselves.

'How do you think I should have my hair done?' Palatine said.

'What shall I wear?' said Isobella. 'He's bound to notice me, of course, but I want to look my best.'

'None of my things are any good,' Palatine said.

They set off that very moment to visit the best dressmaker in Euphrania, only to be told that he had sold out of his entire stock.

'Sold out? What do you mean, you ridiculous man?' the Stepmother said to the unfortunate proprietor. 'How can you be sold out when we haven't purchased anything?'

'The Ball, gracious lady,' the proprietor said. 'I had scarce opened my doors this morning when they descended.'

'Who, who descended?'

'Why, everybody, my lady. They came like the heron to the pool, taking everything I had.'

'I have never heard of such a thing,' the Stepmother said, beside herself with rage by now. 'You, my good man, should learn to distinguish between riff-raff and people of quality like us.'

Her two daughters started to wail and pull faces.

'Oh, Mama, what will become of us?'

'We haven't a thing to wear.'

'Do stop,' their mother exclaimed. 'It spoils your beauty and I'm in a bad enough mood as it is. Coachman, drive home.' She turned to the proprietor. 'Idiot!' she said. He bowed low, content to take such insults while business was so good.

They rushed home again and sorted through their wardrobes, but nothing was to their liking. The Stepmother suddenly had an idea and shouted for Cinderella.

'I have a job for you,' she said. She picked up a bundle of the old dresses and threw them towards the child. 'Unpick these and make three splendid new dresses from them.'

'Oh, Mama,' exclaimed Palatine, 'you're so clever.'

'Make sure they fit to perfection. You can start immediately, there's no time to lose, and you are to work until they're finished.'

'Make sure your hands are clean before you start sewing,' said Isobella.

'And we're to look as pretty as possible,' her sister added. 'Well . . . as pretty as we are.'

Cinderella hurried from the room to begin her new task.

The Prince, too, had to make his own preparations, for although his heart was not in the venture he still had to comply with the protocol of the Court and tradition demanded that he be fitted with a new and magnifi-

cent costume for the Ball. He endured the tailors and fitters with patience, but that patience was fast wearing thin.

'Oh, John, what have I let myself in for?'

'A little more pomp and circumstance . . . and who knows? Perhaps there will be one to whom you can give your heart.'

'Will you dance with your Lady Caroline?' asked the Prince.

'Not done, sire.'

'Oh, yes, I was forgetting. Stupid of me. Where do you meet, if you meet?'

'By the lake, but the opportunities are not many.'

The Prince thought of their separate plights. He went to the window and looked down into the busy courtyard of the palace.

'How absurd life is,' he said. 'Down there, everything is so simple. People meet, fall in love, have children . . . I daresay they envy me here. I'm told envy of princes is a common enough thing . . .'

Cinderella did not have time to envy anybody, let alone princes. She sat in the damp kitchen unpicking and sewing for all she was worth. The dog sat on a stool and watched her. He wagged his tail but she did not notice. He barked but she did not look up.

And when finally, rubbing her tired eyes, she looked around the room for a fresh needle and cotton, the dog had gone.

He left the house, crossed the drawbridge and ran over the fields to a secret hideaway that only he knew about. He had short legs and it took him a long time, and once or twice he was frightened by the great owls who swooped down and flapped ghostly wings about his head. But he was a very brave

dog and he knew that he had to bring help to Cinderella.

After a long time the hideaway came into view. It was an old mill and it stood on the top of a hill. The local inhabitants believed it to be haunted, for the sails of the mill never turned unless there was a full moon.

It wasn't really haunted and, in fact, inside it was very cosy – very untidy, perhaps, but nevertheless cosy. It was the home of the woman who had visited Cinderella, and the reason it was so untidy was that she was such a busy woman she never had time for any cleaning.

On the night in question she was sitting at her desk writing in a large book. It was probably the most untidy desk in the whole world, but the woman never paid much attention to such things. Henrietta, the hen, had made a nest on one corner of the desk because she liked to know what was going on. Above the desk in a wicker cage were the two doves, Hansel and Gretel, and dotted all about were souvenirs of the woman's busy life.

There was a golden apple, for instance, pierced by an arrow, bearing the legend 'With Grateful Thanks From Billy Tell', and beside it a small tree in a pot with a note pinned to it which said, 'From Your Ever Faithful Friends, Marion and Robin Hood,' and beside that a tiny model of a bed with a patchwork quilt on it inscribed, 'Thank You For Waking Me Up – R. V. Winkle.'

Now to a stranger all these things might have seemed very odd indeed, but as you have probably guessed by now, this was no ordinary woman. If the truth were known she had her fingers in a great number of pies.

Like Cinderella she was weary that night. She dipped her pen in the ink once more and finished the story she was writing. Henrietta scratched her head and Hansel and Gretel started to coo, for they were all hungry.

The woman got up to feed them just as the dog arrived.

'Oh, it's you, is it?' said the woman. 'Don't wipe your paws, will you? I've got nobody to help me clean, you know. I have to do it all myself. D'you realize that tiresome Scheherezade is barely half-way through her thousand and one nights? I've got to think of another 496 tales before she's safe, and my diary is chock-a-block.'

She consulted that heavy book on her desk. 'Just look. Wednesday a sea journey to take care of the Little Mermaid, Friday the Ugly Duckling's due to hatch – I have to be back for that – and on Saturday I must get a new key cut for Pandora's Box.'

The dog looked at her and nodded. He had heard it all before, but he had learned never to interrupt. It was better for her to get it off her chest, because afterwards she usually felt sorry and produced a bone.

'It's all very well,' the woman continued, 'for that Hans Christian Andersen to say *his* life is a fairy story . . . Mine

isn't. It's nothing but one long slog. He and those aptly-named Brothers Grimm keep inventing all these characters, but I have to make them work. I can do all manner of things for other people, but never anything for myself. You want a bone? Simple! There you are.'

The juiciest bone any dog could ever imagine was suddenly set before him. Such magic events, which might have confused or troubled certain other dogs, never bothered him. He had long since learned that magic bones usually tasted better than the ones he managed to find behind the butcher's shop. If it pleases her to show off like that, he thought, why should I complain?

'But let me try it for myself,' the woman was saying. 'Would I like a nice cup of tea? Yes, I would. Thank you very much. Now watch this. Kettle . . . Boil!'

The kettle promptly fell off the hob and put the fire out.

'You see? Hopeless! It never works for me. Fairy godmothers ought to have fairy godmothers – the whole system wants a thorough overhaul.'

She rambled on like this for several more minutes and the dog was too polite to interrupt her, although he was getting a little anxious about Cinderella. He chewed on his bone and waited for her monologue to finish.

Unaware that anybody cared about her plight, Cinderella was still hard at work. She had unpicked all the dresses by now and bits and pieces of cloth were scattered all over the kitchen. She had made an attempt to resew some of the pieces into new dresses, but even she could see that the results were awful. Just awful. She could imagine what would happen to her when her Stepmother came to view the results of her labours.

Her fingers were sore from the numerous times she had stuck them with her needle and she was so tired she could hardly see. Of course the fire had gone out and the kitchen was cold. There was nothing to eat and her life seemed a total misery. She put her head on the kitchen table and cried.

She felt a gust of cold wind, but when she looked up the door was closed.

'What's to become of me?' she thought. 'If I don't finish my Stepmother will beat me, and if I do finish she'll find fault with the dresses I've made and still beat me.'

There was a faint rustle behind her and she turned round expecting to see her friends the mice, who usually came out to tidy up the crumbs at this time of night.

Imagine her surprise when she saw the woman sitting by the fire.

'How funny,' she said. 'I was just wishing . . .'

'Yes, I know,' said the woman. She smiled at Cinderella. 'Do you mind if I say something very rude?' She waved a hand towards the half-finished dresses. 'These are hopeless.'

'They're worse than hopeless,' Cinderella agreed. 'I've ruined them and I'm going to get into such trouble.'

'Now, we don't want any of that,' the woman said. 'Dry your tears and have something to eat – you look half-starved and worn out.'

'I'm afraid there isn't anything to eat,' Cinderella sobbed. 'I was too busy doing these to cook anything.'

'What's that then?'

The woman pointed to the table. And there, on the table, was a plate of the most delicious food Cinderella had ever seen.

Her friend the dog had also returned and was sitting by the table, nose in the air, drinking in the intoxicating aroma of the dinner he hoped to share. The bone had only whetted his appetite.

'Where did that come from?'

Cinderella stared at the food and then turned to stare at the woman. She knew it was rude to stare, but she couldn't help herself.

'And where did you come from? I don't understand anything.'

'No, well, very few people do,' the woman said in her matter-of-fact way. 'You're not meant to understand it, you're meant to accept it graciously.'

She got to her feet. 'Look, I'm a very busy woman and I sometimes . . . sometimes . . . lack tact. The first thing you must learn in life is never to go by appearances. Things are never quite what you think they are . . . Do eat up, that's one of my best recipes.'

Cinderella did not need a second bidding. She sat at the table and picked up her knife and fork. The food tasted as delicious as it looked.

'Take me, for example,' the woman said. 'I'm not what I seem. Of course, I don't dress the part, and for very good reason, human nature being what it is . . . Well, I won't go into what I think of human nature, but if I were to go about my business all sparkly and gossamer, quite apart from looking absurd – because despite what they write in those story books for children it's a most unsuitable costume for a grown woman – I'd never be able to sort out the worthy from the unworthy. Don't you agree?'

Cinderella was caught staring again. 'I'm not sure I know what you're talking about,' she said politely.

The woman paused for a moment and looked first towards the stairs and then towards the door. She lowered her voice.

'I'm a . . . fairy godmother. Have been all my life, and don't ask me how I got into it, because it's a long story and highly improbable, and I sometimes wish we'd never been invented.'

'Are there many of you?' Cinderella asked, too amazed to take another mouthful of food.

'Not enough to go round, judging from the amount of work I have to do. However, that's enough of that. I must somehow solve your problem. The best thing you can do is to get a good night's sleep.'

'But how can I go to bed when I haven't finished?'

'Oh, do stop interrupting, and don't give him any more.' She pointed to the dog. 'His eyes are bigger than his stomach. Go along now, do as you're told, and go to bed.'

Cinderella finished the last delicious mouthful and went to her bed in the corner of the kitchen. The woman walked up and down in front of the unfinished dresses.

'What are they wearing in Paris these days? I can't keep up with fashion. Let me concentrate.'

She was still talking to herself when Cinderella closed her eyes. In a few moments she was fast asleep.

It was the dog that woke Cinderella the following morning, and when she had rubbed the sleep from her eyes she saw that the kitchen had once more been transformed.

It was tidy, tidier than she had ever seen it in fact, and standing in one corner on dress forms were three of the most perfect ball gowns that anybody could imagine. The Fairy Godmother had done it again.

Naturally, Cinderella's Stepmother had to find some fault, for she could never give praise without grudging it.

'Yes,' she said, admiring herself in the mirror. 'It isn't what I'm used to, but I must say you've made a reasonable job of the stitching.'

She called for her two daughters to hurry themselves. 'It's time for us to leave and we mustn't keep the Prince waiting.'

The two Step-sisters made their entrance wearing Cinderella's gowns, vainer than ever.

'Mama,' Isobella said in the whining voice she always used when out of temper. 'Mama, I was just telling Palatine that she's not to feel jealous if the Prince asks to dance with me first.'

Palatine pouted. Her face was blotchy with too much powder. 'How do I look, Mama? Don't I look superb?'

'You both look ravishing,' their mother answered, still admiring herself in the mirror. 'It will be difficult for your poor mother to outshine you. Come, let us depart.'

They swept out past Cinderella with their noses in the air. Neither of the two Step-sisters had even said thank you, and their mother's parting remark to Cinderella was merely: 'Clear up the mess in my bedroom. I don't want to come home and find it all untidy.'

Cinderella followed them to the head of the stairs and watched them go outside to the waiting coach.

'Have a nice time,' she said.

'You may depend upon that,' her Stepmother said as the door closed.

Cinderella listened to the sound of the coach clattering over the wooden drawbridge and then went back into the bedroom to begin tidying. She picked up a discarded dress from the floor and then, on a sudden impulse, held it against herself and walked to the mirror.

The reflection only showed a girl dressed in rags, with a smudged face and untidy hair, holding a ball gown, but in her imagination she was one of the Prince's guests at the Ball. She swayed in time to imaginary music and it was as if the Prince held her in his arms as the dance began.

The Prince, to be sure, was already bored. He had been introduced to Her Serene Highness, the Princess Maria of Tuscany, a tall and haughty lady with little to say for herself. He danced a Minuet with her.

Then there was the Grand Duchess Sofia Elizabeth of Dietrichstein, almost as pretty as her portraits suggested, but consumed with her own importance. They danced the first Polonaise together, but all she could talk about was the

superior virtues of her own country compared with Euphrania. The Prince, who was nothing if not good-mannered, suffered in silence.

Next he danced a Polka with Her Imperial Highness Princess Alexandre, a lady of Russian birth who had arrived with an escort of Cossacks, who spoke of nothing but food and how hungry she had been on the long journey to his country. She also trod on his toes.

Of course, whenever he caught his parents' eyes they were smiling and nodding and willing him to make his choice of bride. The Lord Chamberlain was at their side, as anxious as a mother hen, and he felt that everybody in the vast ballroom knew of the decision he had to make and was pitying him. He surveyed the six visiting Princesses with sinking heart, knowing that he was expected to choose, despising himself. He was almost as sorry for them, for they were all pawns in this game of royal marriage chess.

Meanwhile the orchestra played on and it was time for him to take yet another partner onto the floor.

Now it so happened that at this very moment Cinderella's Fairy Godmother was just setting out on another late-night mission. Her journey took her past Cinderella's house. She glanced up at the darkened outline dimly reflected in the waters of the lake. In the distance, beyond the house, she could see the brilliantly illuminated castle where the Ball was taking place.

She stopped, and talked to herself, as she always did when she had a problem to solve.

'Oh, why not?' she said. 'I'll just make time.'

Retracing her steps she hurried across the drawbridge.

Cinderella was back in the kitchen, sitting with the dog by

the side of a miserable fire. The mice were playing on the table.

'Yes, yes, just as I thought. Sitting all alone feeling sorry for ourselves, are we? Well, that's understandable, I suppose – though I never cared much for those Royal occasions myself. Too formal and never enough to eat or drink. Still I daresay that in your heart of hearts you'd like to go.'

'Go? Me . . . go to the Ball?' said Cinderella.

'Well, of course. Isn't that what you were wishing?'

'Not wishing exactly . . . but thinking what it must be like.'

'Comes to the same thing.'

The Fairy Godmother put her basket down and took off her shawl.

'Now, listen,' she said. 'I haven't got a great deal of time because I'm simply run off my feet these days . . . You shall go to the Ball, but I just hope I haven't stretched everything too far and that I can make it work. My powers are not un-limited, you know.'

'No, I didn't know,' said Cinderella.

'I have to share them out. Let me think.'

She blew on the fire while she was thinking and it im-mediately blazed into life.

'Yes,' she said finally. 'I can borrow a bit until midnight.' She looked around and pointed to a pumpkin in one corner of the kitchen.

'Right. You – outside!'

Cinderella watched wide-eyed as the door of the kitchen opened of its own accord and the pumpkin suddenly grew tiny legs and walked outside.

Then the Fairy Godmother turned to the dog.

'I shall need you, and the mice, so take them with you, dog. And see if you can round up a frog or a lizard. Off you go.'

The dog made the mice line up in single file and ushered them outside.

'That's that. Now we must do something about you,

Cinderella. I mean, it's quite obvious you can't go as you are.'

She took one of the empty dress forms and stood it to one side of the fireplace.

'Don't talk to me for a moment, because this doesn't always work and I have to concentrate.'

The fire blazed again and to Cinderella's astonishment a costume suddenly appeared on the dress form. A very odd costume to be sure. A soldier's costume, with a helmet and chain-mail. Cinderella had never been very good at history, but it seemed to her to be a French costume such as Joan of Arc might have worn.

'Oh, dear!' said the Fairy Godmother. 'Oh, dear, oh dear. Most unsuitable.'

She didn't seem too upset, though. In fact she was smiling as she said this.

'Well, I can't think of another magic formula, so you'll just have to go as you are.'

Cinderella tried not to show her disappointment, for she had hoped that the Fairy Godmother would excel herself. She fingered her torn skirt . . . But, wait a minute. What was this? Her skirt wasn't torn. She looked down and found that she was wearing a magnificent dress of rose-pink silk. Now she pinched herself to make sure that she wasn't dreaming. She looked up to find the Fairy Godmother laughing.

'I like pretending I can't do it sometimes,' the Fairy Godmother said. 'It all adds to the fun, magic is so dull when you do it every day of your life.'

Cinderella stood up and danced around the bare kitchen.

'Oh, it's beautiful!' she exclaimed. 'Beautiful! How *do* you do it?'

'Well, that's a trade secret. But it helps if you dream. You see, if you dream . . .'

She moved to another part of the kitchen and picked up an old mop.

'If you dream, suddenly it happens and the dream comes true.'

She twirled the dirty mop and it was immediately transformed into a magnificent silver wig.

Cinderella clapped her hands with joy and suddenly it seemed as though the whole kitchen was filled with bubbles such as fairies float in, and as they burst the wig appeared on her head.

She had scarcely recovered from this when the Fairy Godmother took a large jelly mould from the dresser and turned

it upside down. She poured water from a pitcher into the mould, but it didn't seem like ordinary water, for as it cascaded out of the pitcher it sparkled like silver.

The Fairy Godmother took a plate and, placing it over the jelly mould, turned it again. It seemed to burst into flames and when she lifted it again there, on the plate, was a pair of silver slippers such as no shoemaker had ever made. They seemed so light as to be almost transparent, and they shimmered in the flames of the fire.

Faster than the eye could follow they left the plate and found their way on to Cinderella's feet, and of course they fitted perfectly.

'I can't believe it . . . I can't believe . . . I can't . . .'

She danced around the kitchen while her Fairy God-mother smiled approval.

'Yes, one of my better efforts I think,' said that extra-ordinary lady.

Cinderella stopped in the middle of her dance.

'My Stepmother and Step-sisters . . . they'll recognize me.'

The Fairy Godmother shook her head. 'No one will recognize you for what you are. People seldom do, you know.'

'But how shall I behave? I'm dressed like a princess.'

'Just be yourself. And for tonight, you are a princess – the Princess Incognita. But I must warn you, and take heed for it is a solemn warning . . . the magic I have conjured here tonight is borrowed magic. On the stroke of midnight you must return it, otherwise everything I have transformed will change back to its original state.'

'Everything?'

'Everything. You must be away from the Ball before the last stroke of midnight. Now . . . go and enjoy yourself.'

There were more perfect surprises outside. The mice had become four identical white horses and they waited for Cinderella between the shafts of a golden coach, a coach that changed colours when the moon came out from behind the clouds. Two other mice had changed into footmen fit for a princess, and the frog the dog had found in the bullrushes was now resplendent in the livery of a coachman.

One of the footmen waited to help Cinderella into the coach.

'Thank you, Fairy Godmother,' she managed to say.

'Suddenly it happens to you, Cinderella. Be happy. But don't forget . . . Before the stroke of midnight.'

She stood on the drawbridge and watched the coach disappear towards the distant castle.

'I hope I've done the right thing,' she said to the dog, who was almost as excited as Cinderella. He liked changing mice

and frogs, it was such a relief from chasing boring cats.

'Oh, well,' said the Fairy Godmother, talking to herself again. 'What's done can always be undone. Or so it says in the book. Goodness, but I'm late. If I don't get a move on Ali Baba is going to have an awful time with those forty thieves.'

She was gone before the dog could blink.

The King and Queen, the Lord Chamberlain and indeed the whole Court, to say nothing of the six visiting Princesses and their escorts and ladies-in-waiting, were all looking to the Prince to make his choice. He had danced with all the Princesses, but seemed to favour none. And yet a choice had to be made before the Ball was over, or else there would be a dreadful scandal.

The Queen whispered to the King, who left his Throne and whispered to the Lord Chamberlain, who fingered his neck to make sure his head was still on his shoulders.

There is no telling what would have happened if at that very moment Cinderella had not made her appearance. The assembled guests were suddenly silenced as the Major domo struck his staff of office three times on the floor.

'Your Majesties,' he announced, 'Your Royal Highnesses, My Lords, Ladies and Gentlemen . . . Her Highness the Princess Incognita.'

All eyes turned to the entrance to the Ballroom.

There stood Cinderella, every inch a Princess.

The King looked at the Queen.

The Queen looked at the King.

The Lord Chamberlain said a prayer to himself.

Cinderella looked the length of the Ballroom to where the Prince was standing.

The Prince was as if transfixed. He could not help but stare, even though his royal education had impressed upon him that staring was not the done thing in the best circles.

Nobody moved.

The visiting Princesses gaped . . . yes, gaped, their mouths open. Who was this unknown Princess who had arrived so late? What country did she come from? And where did she get such a magnificent dress?

The orchestra conductor hurriedly sorted through his

music. He had been instructed to play the national anthems for each and every Princess as they arrived, but he could find nothing to fit this unexpected occasion.

Cinderella took the first step towards the Prince. She passed by her Stepmother and her two Step-sisters. They, like the rest of the great assembly, were utterly amazed and perplexed.

'Who can she be?' murmured her Stepmother.

The Prince walked slowly to meet Cinderella in the middle of the vast Ballroom.

The conductor of the orchestra selected his favourite waltz (when in doubt, he had learned from experience, always play a waltz). He tapped with his baton.

As Cinderella and the Prince came together in the centre of the enormous room the first strains of a haunting melody broke the silence.

Cinderella sank down in a deep curtsey in front of the Prince. He motioned her to rise and extended his hand. The

dance commenced, and for a time they danced alone until, as though infected by the Prince's own enchantment, other couples could no longer restrain their happiness and the whole Ballroom became a mass of swirling colour.

The orchestra played as it had never played before, and everybody agreed that the Prince had never looked more handsome and that his unknown partner was an obvious choice for his bride.

The King could hardly contain himself. The moment the waltz had finished the Prince led Cinderella through the ranks of applauding guests to the terrace outside. The King hurried to his puzzled Lord Chamberlain.

'Who can she be?' asked the King.

'I've no idea, Your Majesty. She's not on my list.'

'Your list, your list! Who cares about your list? Find out, man, find out.'

The unfortunate Lord Chamberlain scurried away.

'Play on!' said the King.

'I didn't catch the name,' said the Dowager Queen who had slept through most of the proceedings.

'No, mother, none of us did,' said the King.

'Most irregular,' said the Dowager Queen before her eyes closed again.

I'm sure I seem to you the master of my fate,' the Prince said to Cinderella once they were alone. 'But until this moment I have been a prisoner, trapped by my own birthright.'

Cinderella tried to understand, but she was still so amazed at actually being at the Ball and talking to the Prince that she found it difficult to comprehend anything.

'Trapped?' she said politely.

'Yes. It was never my inclination to behave like this and subject you to this ridiculous charade . . .'

'I think,' said Cinderella, 'I think I should explain why I am here, Your Royal Highness . . .'

'The only evidence I want of you is the evidence of my own eyes . . . and my name is Edward. It is for me to explain myself to you.'

He moved away from her as though in sudden shyness.

'I'm saying all this very badly, but I have always held to the belief that marriage should begin with love . . . I'm sure you agree.'

'I have never given the matter much thought,' said Cinderella truthfully.

'I'm amazed that you even accepted the invitation to the Ball.'

'Yes. I was a little amazed myself.'

'But you still came,' the Prince said. 'Why?'

'Must you ask that?'

'Yes, I must.'

'I had heard . . . much of you.'

'Good or bad?'

'Oh, nothing but good.'

'I can't think how,' said the Prince. 'If I had been you, I'd have believed the worst.'

He took her hands in his. 'You see . . . I was expecting . . . well, I can't tell you what I was expecting. But no matter what happens afterwards I shall always remember this moment, and you must take my present happiness to make you happier. Take it with all my heart, for I give it with all my heart.'

He kissed her tenderly and for the first time in his life he was completely happy.

The enchantment of their meeting was broken by the sudden arrival of the Lord Chamberlain. He coughed dis-

creetly from a distance and bowed low as the Prince turned
at the interruption.

'Yes, what is it?' asked the Prince.

'His Majesty requests an audience of the Princess Incognita, Your Royal Highness.'

'Tell His Majesty we shall be happy to grant his request.'

At that very moment the great clock on the highest tower
of the castle began to strike the hour of midnight. Torn
between her love for the Prince and her promise to her Fairy
Godmother, Cinderella hesitated for a moment, then turned
and fled.

Knowing nothing of the magic, the Prince could only think
of blaming the Lord Chamberlain. 'You frightened her,' he

exclaimed. He ran to the head of the flight of stone stairs, but Cinderella was already out of sight.

She ran like one possessed, while all the time the clock chimed the passing of her new-found happiness. And as she ran her magnificent ball-gown changed back to her rags, leaving only a scattering of rose petals on the stone steps. As she ran, her silver wig faded until, by the time she reached the bottom step, the transformation was complete. The figure that ran across the deserted courtyard found no golden coach to transport her back, only a squashed pumpkin.

The Prince was not quick enough to catch her.

'Wait!' he shouted, 'Come back!' But nobody answered.

Then he saw something glittering at the foot of the steps: a single slipper, and beside it a few scattered rose petals.

He picked it up.

'Come back!' he said again, but the owner of the slipper had vanished, it seemed, without trace.

Cinderella's life resumed its old pattern the following morning. She could dream of the time, a few hours before, when she had danced with the Prince, but now there was work to be done. She was scrubbing and cleaning and drawing water from the well, and there was no magic in that, only drudgery.

'Cinderella!' her Stepmother screamed from the bedroom above. 'Cinderella! Where is the wretched girl?'

Cinderella hurriedly dried her hands and ran upstairs to her Stepmother's bedroom. She found her Stepmother groaning in bed, holding a bottle of smelling salts to her nose.

'Why don't you come when I call you? I want an infusion of weak tea – my head is fit for cracking.'

'Yes, Stepmother.'

Before Cinderella could leave the room her two Stepsisters appeared in the doorway. Their hair was in papers and they both looked a perfect fright.

'Good morning, Mama. Bring us our breakfast immediately, Cinderella.'

'I wasn't able to sleep,' croaked Isobella. 'The excitement of the Ball last night, Mama.'

Palatine collapsed into the nearest chair. 'You would have been amazed,' she said to Cinderella.

Their mother nodded her aching head. 'Your two Stepsisters were a triumph,' she said. 'Had it not been for the late arrival of that mysterious Princess. I feel sure the Prince would have made his choice between my two angels.'

'What Princess was that?' enquired Cinderella in a voice she hoped sounded innocent.

'Nobody seemed to know,' said Isobella.

'The poor Prince seemed very taken with her, but then men always go for the obvious,' Palatine said.

'Yes. I mean, she wasn't *that* pretty, I didn't think. Striking, perhaps. Of course, Mama, I really think the Prince wanted to dance with me. He gave me many a glance. Only natural, I suppose, considering how I looked.'

'You were pleased with your dresses, then?' Cinderella asked.

'Yes,' Isobella said with little grace. 'You did quite a good job. But don't forget our breakfast.'

Cinderella smiled to herself as she hurried from the room.

Palatine stared out of the bedroom window towards the distant castle. 'To think, Mama,' she sighed. 'To think we were actually there, at the castle.'

'Where you belong, my doves.'

'I wonder what the Prince is doing today?'

The Prince was exercising his Royal prerogative for once. He faced his father and the Lord Chamberlain in the Library.

'I'm sick and tired of being treated like some village idiot,' he told them.

'Leave us,' the King said to his Chamberlain.

'No, stay, I want you to hear this. Father, you're the one who treats me like an idiot. You arrange a bride-finding Ball. Against my better judgement I fall in with your plans. I play my part, I'm polite, I greet, I dance with, I flatter, I conceal my boredom from half a dozen twittering maidens of blue blood . . . In short, I fulfil my side of the bargain.'

'True, I can't fault him there,' murmured the King.

'And what happens? I find the lady of my choice and you allow her to disappear into thin air.'

'A search has been made, is being made, Your Royal Highness,' the Lord Chamberlain protested.

'Yes, our police force . . .'

'Our police force, father, couldn't find a missing haystack, let alone a needle . . . How could she have vanished without trace? Do we not have frontiers, Customs posts, guards at every exit from the kingdom?'

'We have Customs, of course,' said the King. 'Valuable source of revenue, and most people say our policemen are wonderful.'

The Prince paused and picked up Cinderella's slipper from the Library table.

'This is apparently the only clue we have, and I found this.'

'Remarkably dainty,' said the King, trying to get his son into a better humour.

'Exactly. It's unique . . . like its vanished owner. Therefore, we must use it. Whoever fits this slipper,' said the Prince, choosing his words carefully, 'must fit the bill.'

The King stared at him. His brain wasn't working very fast that morning.

'He's right. You're right!' he exclaimed. 'Whoever fits tht slipper, shall marry my son.'

'Brilliant!' said the Lord Chamberlain, very relieved that a solution had been found. 'You have solved the problem, Your Majesty.'

'Quite so.'

'A proclamation . . .'

'Draft it,' said the King. 'Let it be known that by Our Royal Command, this slipper . . . it really is very dainty, half the size of your mother's . . . this slipper shall be taken to every stranger of note in the land . . .'

The Prince waited in a fever of anticipation while the search was being made throughout Euphrania.

Old feet, young feet, gnarled feet, feet with bunions, big feet, small feet attempted to claim the slipper as their own. Naturally Cinderella's two Step-sisters demanded their chance, too, but like everybody else they were unsuccessful. As for Cinderella, she was never given an opportunity, and the Royal courier entrusted with the slipper came and went from her house without ever being aware of her existence below stairs.

When the courier returned to the castle he was closely questioned by the Prince. When convinced that the search had been utterly fruitless, the Prince's despair knew no bounds.

'I don't care what anybody says,' he confided to John. 'I know she exists.'

He gave orders for the slipper to be placed inside a glass case set upon a plinth in the main courtyard of the castle.

'It will remain there as a monument to my lost love,' he said.

And remain there it did. At first the curious came from far and wide to stand and stare at it, but gradually as the weeks and months went by and the glass in the case grew dusty, only the Prince and John kept faith.

'Three months, six days, ten hours,' the Prince said. 'That's how long it is since last I saw her . . . What torture love is!'

He and John were out riding and had he but known it he was within half a mile of Cinderella when he said these words. Her life never changed. Confined to the house by her hateful Stepmother, she was kept hard at work from morning till night and the memory of her few hours of happiness at the Ball grew fainter and fainter.

'What torture love is!' the Prince repeated.

'Yes,' said John.

The Prince stared at him. 'How selfish of me! Forgive me, John. In my own unhappiness I was forgetting your plight. Have you seen your Lady Caroline?'

'Yes . . . but infrequently. You see, sire, my father was a servant and my mother the same as he . . .'

'So?'

'So the lady of my choosing is a world away from me.'

'I still don't understand,' said the Prince.

'Position, sire. Position. How you're born and how you're

bred, alas, predetermines whom you wed.'

'John, once before I asked you to excuse my apparent lack of feeling. Are you really telling me that these things still have importance?'

'Yes . . . Oh, yes, that's how it is, sire. And how, I suppose, it always will be.'

The Prince was silent for a moment.

'When I am King I shall alter such things,' he said finally. He seemed to be thinking out aloud. 'But why should I wait until I'm King? Princes, when convinced, should take advantage of *their* position.'

He got down from his horse.

'I can't think why I didn't do something about it before.' He looked up at John and smiled. 'Dismount.'

John did as commanded.

'Kneel,' said the Prince.

John stared at him.

'I command it.'

He unsheathed his sword.

'I dub thee, as it is my privilege so to do, a Knight of the Order of David.' He touched the sword on John's shoulders. 'Arise, Sir John!'

Amazed by the sudden and unexpected turn of events, John got slowly to his feet.

'There!' said the Prince. 'As a Knight of the realm you can now claim the hand of the fair Lady Caroline.'

The realization of his good fortune brought tears to John's eyes. 'What can I say, Your Royal Highness?'

'Nothing. You were my truest friend before, and you are still my truest friend. Go and find her . . . Go now and be happy . . .'

John needed no second bidding. The Prince watched him ride off into the distance.

'Be happy enough for both of us,' the Prince said. .

He returned to the castle and stood before the glass case

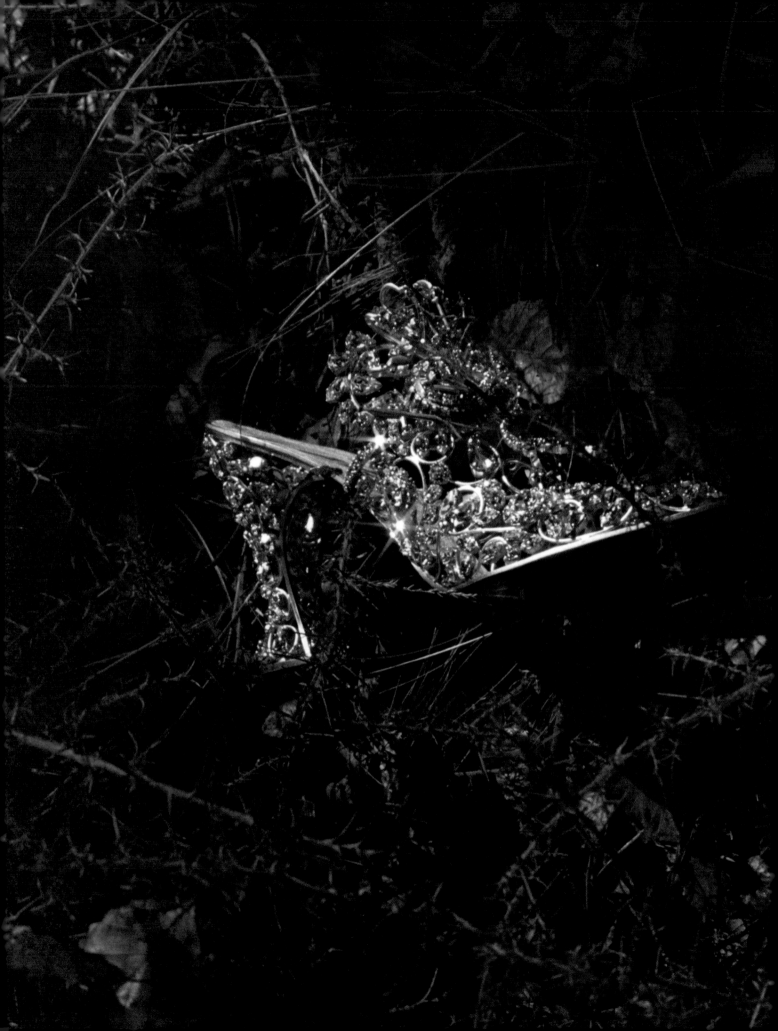

containing the slipper. He stood there for a long time, wondering why fortune refused to smile upon him. Then, while the Guards stood stiffly to attention, he smashed the glass with his gloved hand and removed the slipper. He looked at it one last time, then flung it over the castle battlements.

It came to rest amongst the thorns and bracken at the foot of the castle walls, and there it lay, forgotten.

Much of life is a matter of chance, and it so happened that a short time after the events we have just described, Cinderella's dog paid a visit to the castle. Because he was a mere dog most people would imagine that he went there to scrounge a bone from the royal kitchens, but some of us know differently. Whether by accident or design, his route to the kitchens took him past the spot where Cinderella's slipper lay hidden. He stopped. His nose went into the air. He sniffed, he scratched around and he un-covered the slipper. Being the dog he was, he immediately forgot all thoughts of juicy bones and ran in search of his mistress.

He made such a fuss when he found her, tugging at the frayed hem of her dress, running round in circles and barking, that she felt compelled to follow him and find out what all the excitement was about.

He led her back to the foot of the castle walls, back to the very spot where the slipper was hidden. Cinderella could not believe her eyes. Holding the slipper up into the sunlight, she danced across the fields. The dog shared her happiness, racing ahead of her and turning somersaults, which he did rather well for the Fairy Godmother had once made him join a circus.

Then chance intervened again, for John and Lady Caroline,

who were now able to meet quite freely, were wandering hand in hand across these same meadows. It was John who first caught sight of Cinderella. He recognized her, of course, and his eyes were dazzled as the sun glinted on the magic slipper.

'We must fetch the Prince,' he said, and he and Lady Caroline ran to their horses and galloped off back to the castle.

Cinderella danced on in the field of tall grass and it was there that the Prince found her again. He rode in on his white stallion and claimed her, for Princes always do things in style.

'Now that I've found you,' he said, 'I shall never lose you again.'

Together they went to confront Cinderella's Stepmother. You can imagine how dumbfounded that lady was in the presence of the Prince. As for her two daughters, they immediately collapsed with shock.

'I little knew, Madam, that I should have the pleasure of meeting you and your daughters again in such happy circumstances.'

The Stepmother finally found her tongue. 'What . . . circumstances . . . Your Royal Highness?'

'You are the legal guardian, I believe, of my wife-to-be?'

'Your wife-to-be? Why, yes, of course . . . I am more than her legal guardian . . . I have been a mother to her.'

'Indeed, Madam,' said the Prince, who was thoroughly enjoying himself, having been told of the true situation by Cinderella. 'Then I do right by formally asking your permission to take Cinderella's hand in marriage?'

This was too much for Cinderella's Step-sisters. They wailed and moaned and lurched like two old hens. 'Will you be quiet!' snapped their mother. She forced a smile to her lips as she answered the Prince, for she was already thinking how to turn this unwelcome news to her own advantage.

'Permission? Well, of course, gladly. Please, Your Royal

Highness, allow me the honour of inviting you into our happy home . . . Cinderella, dear, we were so worried about you.'

But the Prince answered for them both. 'Thank you, but no. I have other urgent business to attend to.'

The Stepmother and her daughters sank into a deep curtsey as the Prince led Cinderella back across the drawbridge. They paused there and Cinderella turned.

'In my happiness,' she said, 'I forgive you all.'

The moment they had departed the Stepmother's true character showed itself again. She rounded on her two daughters, slapping their wrists with her fan.

'Forgive me!' she stormed. 'How dare she forgive me! Oh, the humiliation of it all . . .'

'Come closer, my child. What did you say your name was?' the King enquired.

Cinderella stood beside her Prince in front of the entire Court. The King, the Queen and the Dowager Queen were seated on their magnificent thrones. Beside them were the Ladies-in-Waiting, the Ministers and, of course, the Lord Chamberlain.

'Cinderella, Your Majesty.'

'A most unusual name,' the Queen observed without a smile.

'The name, mother, is surely of no importance,' her son answered. 'All that matters is that I have made my choice and wait for your blessings.'

'You caused us a lot of trouble, you know,' said the King. 'After the Ball people were looking for you everywhere. You vanished, you see. Did you go back to your own kingdom?'

'No, Your Majesty. I went back to where I live.'

'And where is that, child?' asked the Queen.

'Why, here, Your Majesty.'

'Here?' said the King, completely puzzled. 'In the castle?'

'No, father,' laughed the Prince. 'As you have often remarked, love is blind and we sometimes don't look under our own noses. Cinderella lives in our own Euphrania not twenty miles from here.'

'Who is this girl?' said the Dowager Queen, who was suddenly aware of a disturbance in her normal routine. 'Why doesn't somebody tell me what is going on?'

'This is the girl that Edward wants to marry,' said the King in a loud voice, for his mother was somewhat hard of hearing.

'Is going to marry, father,' said the Prince with some emphasis.

'Well, I don't wish to sound offensive,' the Dowager Queen continued, 'but she seems most unsuitably dressed for such a solemn occasion.'

'You are quite right, grandmama. It is something I shall correct immediately. Father . . . by your leave.'

The Prince bowed and led Cinderella from the Throne Room. He intended to instruct the Royal dressmakers to prepare a complete wardrobe for Cinderella, since she had no fine clothes of her own and was still dressed in her rags.

Behind them in the Throne Room the King left his throne and motioned for the Lord Chamberlain to follow him. Their heads were bent together and both had worried expressions.

That night the Prince shared his happiness with his good friend John. 'To think,' he said, 'that tonight she sleeps within the castle walls, safe at last . . . Nothing can stand in our way now. Nothing.'

John nodded his agreement, but secretly he had doubts,

for he had seen the King's face in the Throne Room and he knew of the rumours that the Star Council of Ministers had been summoned to a special and secret meeting.

John's premonitions, alas, were all too real.

Later that same night, when the castle was silent, the Lord Chamberlain made his way along the candlelit corridors to the door of Cinderella's chamber.

He knocked on the door.

Within the chamber Cinderella was still awake, for the excitement of the day's events had driven all thoughts of sleep from her happy head. She sat up in the enormous four-poster bed.

'Who is it?'

'My lady, His Majesty the King has commanded me to request an audience of you.'

It seemed a somewhat unusual request to make in the middle of the night, but then everything about her new life seemed strange. She slipped out of bed and put on a gown of the finest silk which formed part of the magnificent wardrobe the Prince had provided for her. Then she was ready to receive the Lord Chamberlain.

He bowed to her from the door.

'My apologies for disturbing your rest, but, alas, there are some matters of state that cannot be delayed.'

He came closer, and now she could see that his face was troubled.

'His Majesty has asked me, as his principal Minister, to broach a subject of some delicacy . . .'

He seemd very nervous for some reason.

'You love the Prince Edward, do you not?'

'Why, of course,' Cinderella said. 'Who wouldn't?'

'Quite so, quite so . . . And he has professed his love for you to the whole Court.'

'Yes. Yes, he has.'

Such strange and obvious questions to ask, thought

Cinderella, but still she had no inkling of what was to come.

'Very commendable,' the Lord Chamberlain said.

His lined old face seemed to crumble and he turned away as though unable to meet her unsuspecting eyes.

'Oh, dear, oh, dear!' he said, and he sounded very tired. 'I'm really too old for this sort of thing. Forgive me, my dear child, but despite my appearance and the pomp and circumstance of my high office, I am not without understanding of your plight . . . for plight it is.'

He took both her hands and guided her to a chair.

'To be blunt, for the hour is late . . . It is not possible for His Majesty to give consent to such a marriage.'

At first Cinderella imagined that she had misheard him. Then she imagined that she was really asleep and that this was all a nightmare. What the Lord Chamberlain was saying could not be true.

'Not possible? What does that mean, what are you saying, my Lord?'

'Your love for the Prince, and his for you, well, that is a fine and private thing and would that it could remain so . . . but the times demand something different. The Prince must make a marriage of alliance to a Princess of the blood royal . . . And that is why I am here, burdened with this unhappy task.'

He searched for the right words to soften the final blow.

'You see, my dear child, in life love cannot always find a way . . . You were born here and so you know that our little kingdom, whilst far from perfect, has yet enjoyed many centuries of peace. That peace is now threatened from without – there are some who look towards our frontiers with greedy eyes. You see only love and happiness staring you in the face . . . I see nothing but war and destruction, unless a sacrifice is made . . .'

'And the sacrifice is to be me . . .'

The Lord Chamberlain nodded. 'It is a lot to ask, but I must ask it.'

'To leave him now . . . ?'

'To leave him now . . . before it is too late.'

'But how would I do that?' Cinderella cried. 'He would search for me again. He would search for me and find me, I know he would.'

'Yes, that too is true,' the Lord Chamberlain agreed. 'But we have allowed for that. It is suggested that . . . with proper dowry and every other consideration fitting the circumstances of this most unhappy occasion . . . It is suggested that you be taken from here this very night to a secret place of exile far beyond our borders . . .'

'You have forgotten nothing then,' Cinderella managed to say. She struggled to restrain her tears. The dream had turned into nightmare. She realized that pleading was no use, for despite his tact and understanding the Lord Chamberlain had to carry out his task without pity. She saw his face as a blur in the candlelit room heavy with the scent of roses. He was talking to her again, and his words came to her as though through a fog.

'If you love the Prince Edward, as I am sure you do, my lady, think of him as the future King and your sacrifice will not have been in vain . . .'

'Yes,' she whispered, with sudden dignity, a dignity beyond her years. 'You need say no more . . . you were well chosen for the task . . . But in bowing to the Royal demand, I must make one of my own . . .'

'My lady . . . ?'

'It is not very much, and something which, with your greater experience in these matters, you will not find difficult . . . I wish you to tell His Royal Highness . . . Prince Edward . . . I wish you to tell him . . .'

It was no use. Her courage finally failed her.

'Tell him anything,' she said, 'but not that I love him . . .'

In the dead of night, with only the King's personal bodyguard as witnesses, she was escorted through the silent castle to an inner courtyard. There a coach and escort awaited her. The Lord Chamberlain kissed her hand and took his leave. The coach moved out into the darkness and soon was lost to sight.

High above the courtyard the King watched the departure from a darkened window in the library. He stood there for a while thinking of his own lost youth.

Shortly afterwards he was joined by the Lord Chamberlain. That gentleman seemed to have aged like his sovereign, for they were both good men at heart, but they had a destiny to fulfil.

The Lord Chamberlain bowed. 'Your Majesty,' he said, 'the deed is done.'

The King sighed and looked down once more into the deserted courtyard.

'She certainly *behaved* like a Princess,' he said.

The next morning when the Prince discovered what had taken place his anger and anguish knew no bounds. He gave orders for a troop of his cavalry to be saddled and give chase, and he himself led them with John at his side. They rode like the wind with swords drawn until they reached the border. But they were too late. For the second time in his life Cinderella had vanished without trace.

He returned to the castle and confronted his father.

'You have done what you have done,' he said, 'and the spoils are yours, but it is a small victory.'

'If I could explain . . .' said the King.

'No. Spare me that. Spare me the final hypocrisy of your sympathy. Take your map, rearrange it to your heart's content, make your precious marriage of alliance . . . You have destroyed whatever vestige of love and happiness I might have found and you have done it in the name of patriotism . . . So let it be thus.'

Knowing the justice of his son's bitter accusation, the King could make no defence.

'Choose me a bride from amongst that rag-bag of royal virgins I have twice rejected,' the Prince continued. 'Choose who you will, for I care not. I will play my public part to the altar, but no further. Your Royal House will live with you, but die with me.'

And so with no rejoicing in the land, the preparations for the wedding went ahead. The Prince spoke to nobody but John. At night he did not sleep, but paced his room from one corner to the other until those about him feared he would lose his reason. He commanded that every day a single red rose be brought to his room and placed alongside the silver slipper which rested on a velvet cushion by his bed.

On the day of the wedding ceremony he went alone to the private chapel in the castle and knelt in his ceremonial robes to pray.

'Dearest Cinderella, forgive me. I have no heart for what I must shortly perform, for my heart is yours and yours alone. It is only in fairy tales that a Prince marries the lady of his choice . . . The real world is not so kind. I have loved but once, I have loved but you, and I have lost you twice . . .'

Cinderella, in a distant land, was unaware of such events. She lived the life of a recluse, with every comfort but one and wealth enough to buy everything but happiness. She could only dream of what might have been.

Our story might have ended there, but for Cinderella's dog. The moment his mistress disappeared he set out on a long journey to find the Fairy Godmother. He was a small dog, as you know, and couldn't travel very fast, but for all that he didn't lack courage and refused to give up hope. Remembering the dates in the Fairy Godmother's diary, he visited the Ugly Duckling first. She had hatched and in fact had already turned into a beautiful swan. Then he swam a large lake and

followed a river to where it met the sea. There he found the Little Mermaid, but all she could tell him was that the Fairy Godmother had been and gone. He journeyed on to Pandora's house; she gave him food and another address of an old lady who for some reason lived in a shoe. *She* directed him to a forest and told him to ask for a little girl called Red Riding Hood. On the way he met a wolf, and although in normal circumstances he was not afraid of wolves he daren't risk being delayed any longer, but sped on until he came to Aladdin's cave and there he found her. She didn't recognize him at first, because by now his coat was ragged and dusty. She gave him a bath (which he hated) and a bowl of her magic soup (which he adored) and made him tell her the whole story.

'Well, I'm not having that,' she said.

She rubbed Aladdin's lamp and the genie appeared.

87

'Now, I don't want any trouble from you,' she said. 'Just tell me where Cinderella is and be quick about it, otherwise I shall take all your powers away.'

The genie wasn't too happy taking orders from a woman, and thought how the world had changed since he had first been trapped within the lamp. He huffed and puffed a little, mostly for his own dignity, and then gave her the directions. Gathering up the weary dog, the Fairy Godmother caught the next flying carpet and was off.

They landed in the garden of Cinderella's secret hideaway.

'Goodness, you gave me such a shock! Cinderella exclaimed.

'I should hope so. It's nothing to the shock you gave me. You shouldn't be here at all, that's not how I planned it. Really, I sometimes wish I could retire. Unless I'm on the spot to take care of every little detail, something always goes wrong. I know exactly what happened . . . You stayed beyond the stroke of midnight, didn't you?'

'Yes,' Cinderella said. 'But please don't scold me, I'm unhappy enough as it is.'

'Of course you're unhappy. Any girl would be unhappy if she's missing her own wedding.'

'Wedding?'

'Yes. The Prince gets married today. I have the date underlined in my diary.'

'Who . . . who is he marrying?'

'Well, at the moment, the wrong girl, obviously. Oh, it's too irritating. I had it all mapped out. Still, I suppose I shall have to rise to the occasion again and do something spectacular. Spectaculars always take so much out of me. So, come along, we haven't got a moment to lose.'

'But you can't change anything now,' Cinderella said. 'I'm not allowed to marry him.'

'Who says so?'

'The King.'

'Oh, fiddlesticks. One must never be awed by Kings. In all my career I've made it a firm rule to totally ignore the whims of royalty. Good gracious me, I'd *have* to retire if that was the case. I once had an Emperor take off all his clothes . . . one of my finest moments.'

'But how will you do it?'

'Don't ask stupid questions, just come with me. It was the same with Snow White – never do as you're told, you young girls. Men are much easier to deal with.'

The wedding had already begun.

The Prince and the Princess chosen as his bride-to-be stood in front of the High Altar of the Cathedral.

Included in the vast congregation were many crowned heads of visiting royalty. The solemn and elaborate ritual befitting the wedding of the heir to the throne was an occasion to be endured rather than enjoyed.

Nobody noticed the sudden arrival of the Fairy God-mother. She had dressed herself in a gown of such magnificence that it rivalled those of the watching nobility around her.

Once in her seat, she gave the signal for Cinderella to enter through the great West door of the cathedral. If the Palace Guards thought there was anything odd about the arrival of a second bride, they gave no sign, for they were too well trained and disciplined.

The Fairy Godmother winked at Cinderella to give her encouragement. Secretly she congratulated herself, for she really had done a marvellous job in the time. No bride could ever have looked lovelier. Her wedding dress had been woven from the threads of a thousand legends, and as she moved slowly to the centre of the aisle it was as though she was surrounded by the light of the midsummer moon.

And yet . . . and yet there was something missing. For a moment or two the Fairy Godmother couldn't remember what. She concentrated very hard. A fanfare! That was it. Every royal bride was always introduced by a fanfare.

She whispered one of her most potent spells and seconds later a trumpet made of the finest glass appeared in her lap.

She raised it to her lips and the voice of the old Archbishop who was conducting the wedding service was suddenly obliterated by the sound of the magic trumpet.

All heads turned and a great murmur rippled through the assembly as they saw Cinderella standing in the shaft of light.

The Archbishop faltered.

The Princess bride turned to her father, the ruler of Carolsfeld.

He looked at the King of Euphrania, who – as baffled as anybody – turned to the Lord Chamberlain. That worried man had nobody to turn to. He could only gasp.

Prince Edward was the last to turn his head and when he saw his beloved Cinderella there could be no doubt in anybody's mind as to the final outcome. Nor was there any hesitation in his step as he left his place in front of the altar and walked to meet Cinderella.

In full view of the whole congregation they were reunited. You can imagine the commotion. The Princess from Carolsfeld promptly fainted and the Dowager Queen woke up.

'Is the ceremony over?' she enquired in a very loud voice. 'What a relief!'

The majority of those present did not share such relief. The two royal families and their entourages retired into the vestry so that dignity could be restored in private.

The Lord Chamberlain paced to and fro with his angry monarch.

'You realize, Your Majesty, this could mean war,' he said.

'I know, I know,' snapped the King. 'Well, think of something.'

'He cannot marry this girl, sire, the Constitution doesn't allow it.'

'Don't tell me,' said the King. 'I wrote it.'

'Yes, don't tell him, he wrote it,' the Fairy Godmother interrupted, having just made one of her magic appearances.

'I beg your pardon, my lady,' the Lord Chamberlain said.

'And if he wrote it, he can unwrite it.' She turned to the King and gave him a smile which almost melted his crown.

'After all, you are the King,' she said.

'That's right, I am.'

'And absolute monarchs should act absolutely. It's very becoming.'

'She's right,' agreed the King. He took the Lord Chamberlain to one side. 'Who is she?'

'I've no idea, Your Majesty. Probably one of the visitors.

But that doesn't solve the problem. Even if you do change the Constitution, there still remains the question of the other bride.'

'You're right.' The bewildered King looked to the Fairy Godmother. 'He's right. We're back to where we started.'

'It's staring you in the face,' the Fairy Godmother said.

'What is?'

'The answer.'

She indicated for him to look across the crowded room. Cousin Montague and the Princess from Carolsfeld were holding hands and staring intently at each other. They were so still they might have been in a waxworks.

'What sort of answer is that?' asked the King.

'They're in love.'

'They are?'

'You have my word for it,' said the Fairy Godmother, who knew a perfect match when she arranged one. 'It was love at first sight.'

The King stared.

'Ask him,' the Fairy Godmother prompted.

Hardly believing his good fortune, the King approached his hitherto unfavourite relative.

'Cousin,' he said hesitantly. 'Cousin, it has been brought to my notice . . .'

'Oh, yes, and to mine,' sighed Cousin Montague. 'Isn't she ravishing?'

'But am I to understand . . . ?'

'Yes, anything,' said the bewitched Montague.

He took the Princess in his arms without a thought for the protocol of the Court and embraced her.

The Bride's father and mother gasped. Several members of their entourage visibly wilted, shocked beyond belief.

. Making a valiant attempt to keep the smile of relief off his face, the King crossed the room to his fellow monarch.

'As fathers,' he said, 'what can we do?'

'It's a question of honour,' said the ruler of Carolsfeld. He looked as though he might choke on the spot.

'Well it seems to be a . . .' Words failed the King in his moment of victory.

'Fait accompli?' suggested the Lord Chamberlain, who liked to parade his few words of French.

'It's certainly a fate,' ventured the King, but the joke misfired. Recovering, he tried to look dignified.

'What do you suggest?' thundered the other King.

The Fairy Godmother, who was of course listening to the entire conversation, put the remaining words into both their mouths.

'Well, it looks like another wedding,' said the King.

'The sooner the better. My place, I think. I'll arrange it all.'

The King clasped him round his shoulders.

'Thus cementing our great alliance,' he proclaimed.

'Concealing our shame,' answered his royal companion.

Cinderella and Prince Edward were duly married. The Fairy Godmother and her dog stayed long enough to witness the exchange of rings, and then she was off again to right other wrongs and make other wishes come true. She's still around somewhere, although she doesn't visit Euphrania very often. She doesn't have to, you see, because that tiny kingdom, which takes some finding on the map, is that rare part of the world that always enjoys peace and happiness. Most of her time she tries to make people see that love is better than hate. She doesn't always succeed, but she keeps trying. So spare her a thought, for as long as somebody is trying, there's always the hope that one day it might come true.

Chosen for
The Royal Film Performance 1976

in the gracious presence of
Her Majesty Queen Elizabeth the Queen Mother

Odeon Theatre Leicester Square
Wednesday 24th March

To aid the Cinema and Television
Benevolent Fund

Paradine Co-Productions Limited
present

The Slipper and the Rose
The Story of Cinderella

Richard Chamberlain Gemma Craven
as The Prince   as Cinderella

Annette Crosbie Edith Evans Christopher Gable
as The Fairy Godmother   as The Dowager Queen   as John

Michael Hordern Margaret Lockwood Kenneth More
as The King   as The Stepmother   as The Lord Chamberlain

Production Co-ordinators Naim Attallah and John Asprey Executive Producer David Frost

Music and Lyrics Richard M. Sherman and Robert B. Sherman Music arranged and conducted by Angela Morley Choreographer Marc Breaux

Screenplay by Bryan Forbes and Robert B. Sherman Richard M. Sherman

Produced by Stuart Lyons Directed by Bryan Forbes

Panavision® Technicolor® Distributed by Cinema International Corporation

Original Soundtrack Album on E.M.I. EMC 3116.